James A. Froude

Luther

A Short Biography

James A. Froude

Luther
A Short Biography

ISBN/EAN: 9783337126797

Printed in Europe, USA, Canada, Australia, Japan

Cover: Foto ©Raphael Reischuk / pixelio.de

More available books at **www.hansebooks.com**

L U T H E R :

A SHORT BIOGRAPHY.

BY

JAMES ANTHONY FROUDE, M.A.

HONORARY FELLOW OF EXETER COLLEGE,
OXFORD.

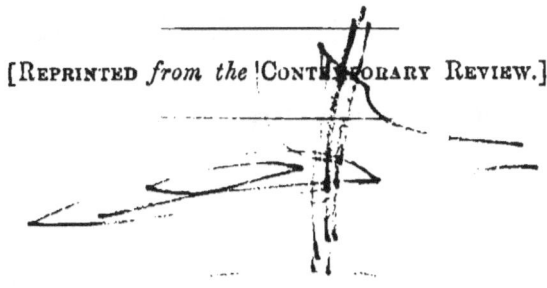

[Reprinted *from the* Contemporary Review.]

LONDON:

LONGMANS, GREEN, AND CO.

1883.

PREFACE.

In the coming winter Protestant Germany will celebrate the four hundredth anniversary of the birth of Martin Luther. Princes, statesmen, soldiers, men of letters, the Emperor himself, men of all ranks and all professions, will unite in doing honour to the memory of the miner's son, whom they regard as their spiritual liberator. Such a movement, at a period when we hear much of the Catholic revival, is a sign of the times, and a remarkable one. When the German States revolted against the Roman hierarchy, we in England revolted also; but there is no name, among the English apostles of the Reformation, which commands the same respect as Luther's. Knox holds a position something like it in Scotland: Presbyterian Scotland is Knox's work, and the people know this and feel it. But even the Scots do not observe Knox's birthday. Not many of them, probably, could tell either the day or the year in which he came into the world. The great English Reformers, well as they deserved of us, stand in far lower esteem. For various reasons they have never been extremely honoured, and in these days seem less in favour than ever they were.

Nevertheless, we are still a Protestant nation, and the majority of us intend to remain Protestant. If we are indifferent to our Smithfield and Oxford martyrs, we are not indifferent to the Reformation, and we can join with Germany in paying respect to the memory of a man to whom we also, in part, owe our deliverance. Without Luther there would have been either no change in England in the sixteenth century, or a change purely political. Luther's was one of those great individualities which have modelled the history of mankind, and modelled it entirely for good. He revived and maintained the spirit of piety and reverence in which, and by which alone, real progress is possible.

The English people, therefore, will not look on indifferent upon this occasion, as on a thing with which they have no concern. Germany takes the first place in the celebration, because Luther was a son of her own. But he belongs not to Germany alone, but to the human race; and this little book is published that English readers may have before them in a comprehensive form the chief features of Luther's actions and character.

LUTHER.[1]

————◦◦◦————

AT LAST we have a Life of Luther which deserves the name. Lives there have been many in various languages, and Collections of Letters, and the Table Talk, and details more or less accurate in Histories of the Reformation; but a biography which would show us Luther in all aspects—as a child, as a man, as the antagonist of Popes and Princes, and as a father and householder in his own home, as he appeared to the world, and as he appeared to his wife and children and his personal friends —for such a biography Europe has waited till the eve of the four hundredth anniversary of his birth. The greatest men, strange to say, are those of whom the world has been contented to know the least. The 'lives' of the greatest saints of the Church are little more than legends. A few pages will contain all that can be authentically learnt of Raphael or Shakspeare.

Of Luther, at all events, this can no longer be said. Herr Köstlin in a single well-composed volume has produced a picture which leaves little to be desired. A student who has read these 600 pages attentively will

[1] *Luthers Leben.* Von Julius Köstlin. Leipzig, 1883. An English translation of this book has just been published by Messrs. Longmans and Co.

have no questions left to ask. He will have heard Luther
speak in his own racy provincial German. He will have
seen him in the pulpit. He will have seen him in Kings'
Courts and Imperial Diets. He will have seen him at
his own table, or working in his garden, or by his
children's bedside. He will have seen, moreover—and it
is a further merit of this most excellent book—a series
of carefully engraved portraits from the best pictures, of
Luther himself, of his wife and family, and of all the
most eminent men with whom his work forced him into
friendship or collision.

Such a volume is singularly valuable to us, now
especially, when the forces of the great spiritual deep are
again broken up ; when the intellect, dissatisfied with
the answers which Luther furnished to the great problems
of life, is claiming on one side to revise those answers,
and his great Italian enemy, whom he and the Protestant
world after him called Antichrist, is pretending on the
other that he was right after all, and that we must believe
in him or in nothing. The Evangelicals are faint-hearted.
The men of science are indifferent. The Romanists see
their opportunity of revenging themselves on the memory
of one who in life wrought them so much woe and shame ;
and had no such effort been made, Luther's history would
have been overgrown, like a neglected grave, with the
briars and nettles of scandal. The philosophy of history
undervalues the work of individual persons. It attri-
butes political and spiritual changes to invisible forces
operating in the heart of society, regarding the human
actors as no more than ciphers. It is true that some
great spiritual convulsion would certainly have shaken
Europe in the sixteenth century, for the Papal domin-
ation was intellectually and morally undermined ; but

the movement, inevitable as it was, might have lasted a hundred years, and the results might have been utterly different. If it had been left to Erasmus and the humanists, the shell of Romanism might have survived for centuries, while a cultivated Epicureanism took the place of real belief and dissolved the morality of mankind. If the revolt had been led by fanatics like Carlstadt, or Zwingle, or Münzer, the princes of the Empire would have combined to drown an insurrection in blood which threatened the very existence of society. [That the Reformation was able to establish itself in the shape which it assumed was due to the one fact that there existed at the crisis a single person of commanding mind as the incarnation of the purest wisdom which then existed in Germany, in whose words the bravest, truest, and most honest men saw their own thoughts represented; and because they recognised this man as the wisest among them, he was allowed to impress on the Reformation his own individuality.] The traces of that one mind are to be seen to-day in the mind of the modern world. Had there been no Luther, the English, American, and German peoples would be thinking differently, would be acting differently, would be altogether different men and women from what they are at this moment.

The Luders, Luthers—the same name as Lothair—were a family of peasants at Möhra or More, a village on the skirts of the Thuringian forest, in the Electorate of Saxony. 'I am a peasant's son,' Luther wrote; 'father, grandfather, greatgrandfather, were all peasants.' The father, Hans or John, was a miner. He learnt his trade in a copper mine at Möhra, but removed in early manhood to Eisleben, where business was more active; and there, being a tough, thrifty, industrious man, he did well for himself. The Möhra people were a hard race —what the Scotch call 'dour'—and Hans Luther was one of them. He married a peasant woman like himself, and from this marriage, now just 400 years ago, on the 10th of November, 1483, came into the world at Eisleben his first-born son Martin.

Six months later, still following his mining work, Hans moved his family to Mansfeld, a few miles distant, in a valley on the slopes of the Hartz mountains. He continued to prosper. He worked himself with his pick in the mine shafts. The wife cut and carried the wood for the cottage. Hans, steadily rising, became the proprietor of a couple of smelting furnaces; in 1491 he became one of the four Church elders—what we should call churchwardens. He drew the attention of Count Mansfeld himself, whose castle overhung the village, and was held in high esteem by him. Melanchthon, who knew both Hans and his wife, admired and honoured both of them. Their portraits were taken afterwards by Cranach—the features of both expressing honesty, piety, and clear intelligence. Martin was the eldest of seven children; he was brought up kindly, of course, but without special tenderness. He honoured and loved his parents, as he was bound to do, but he thought in his own later life that they had been over-harsh with him. He remembered that he had been beaten more than once for trifles, worse than his fault deserved.

Of the village school to which he was early sent his recollections were only painful. He was taught to read and write, and there was what pretended to be an elementary Latin class. But the schoolmasters of his childhood, he said, were jailers and tyrants; and the schools were little hells. A sense of continued wretchedness and injustice weighed on him as long as he remained there, and made his childhood miserable. But he must have shown talents which encouraged his father to spare no cost on his son's education that his own scanty means would allow. When he was fourteen he was sent to a more expensive school at Magdeburg, and thence, after a year, to a still better school at Eisenach, where he was taught thoroughly well, and his mind began to open. Religion, as with all superior lads, became the first thought with him. He asked himself what God was, what he was, and what God required him to do; and here the impressions of his home experiences began to weave themselves into what he learnt from books.

The old Hans was a God-fearing man, who prayed habitually at his children's bedside; but he was one of those straightforward people who hated arguments about such things, who believed what he had been told by his priest, but considered that, essentially, religion meant the leading a good life. The Hartz mountains were the home of gnomes and demons, or at least of the popular belief in such things. Such stories Father Luther regarded as lies or tricks of the devil; but the devil himself was a grave reality to him; while the mother believed in witches, and was terribly afraid of them. Hans himself could see straight into a good many things. He was very ill once. The parish priest came to prepare him for death, and suggested that he should leave a legacy to the Church. Hans answered, 'I have many children; I will give what I have to them; they need it more.' He had something of his son's imagination. Looking one day over a harvest field, Martin heard him say, 'How strange to think of the millions of men and women eating and drinking all over the earth—and all to be gathered into bundles like those cornstalks.' Many such speeches young Martin must have remembered and meditated on. He had a happy life on the whole at this school at Eisenach. He is described as having been a merry quick young fellow, fond of German proverbs and popular songs and stories. He had a passion for music, and helped out the cost of his education by singing carols at night from door to door with three or four companions. A Frau von Cotta, the wife of a rich Eisenach gentleman, took notice of him on these occasions, made acquaintance with him, and invited him to her house.

His promise was still great. His father, who had no leanings for priestcraft, designed him rather for the law than the Church, and when he was eighteen sent him to Erfurt, which was then the best university in Germany. It was the period of the revival of learning; scholastic pedantry was deposed from the throne where it reigned so long, and young men were beginning to breathe freely, in the fresh atmosphere of Ovid and Virgil and Cicero. Luther rose rapidly by the ordinary steps, became Baccalaureus and Magister, and covered himself on the way with distinction. He attended law lectures and waded into the *Corpus Juris*; but desires were growing in him which these studies failed to satisfy. In the University library he found, by accident, a Latin Bible which opened other views of what God required of him. He desired to be good, and he knew that he was not good. He was conscious of ambition, pride, vanity, and other young men's passions, of which the Bible told him to cure himself. He was not a man in whom impressions could be lightly formed, and lightly lost; what he felt he felt intensely. His life had been innocent of any grave faults, but he was conscious every moment of

many little ones. 'Alas!' he said one day when he
was washing his hands, 'the more I wash them, the
fouler they grow.' The loss of an intimate friend
brought vividly before him the meaning of death and
judgment. The popular story of the young Alexius, said
to have been killed at his side by lightning, is, in itself, a
legend; but the essence of it is true. Returning to
Erfurt, in the summer of 1505, from a visit to his family
at Mansfeld, he was overtaken by a storm. The lightning struck the ground before his feet; he fell from his
horse. 'Holy Anne,' he cried to the mother of the
Virgin, 'help me; I will become a monk.' Next day at
Erfurt he repented of his vow, for he knew how it would
grieve his father; but his life had been spared; he
believed that the vow had been heard and registered
in heaven; and without waiting for his resolution to
be shaken, he sought, and found admittance in the
Augustinian monastery in the town. His career
hitherto had been so brilliant that the old Hans had
formed the brightest hopes for him. He was bitterly dis-
appointed, knowing, perhaps, more of monks and monk-
dom than his son. He consented with a sore heart,
perhaps hoping that a year's experience and the discipline of the novitiate would cure a momentary folly.
The Augustinians owned no property; they lived on
alms, and the young Martin, to break his pride, was set
to the lowest drudgery in the house, and was sent about
the town to beg. Luther, however, flung himself with
enthusiasm into the severest penances. He fasted, he
prayed, he lay on the stones, he distracted his spiritual
adviser with the refinements of his confessions. The
common austerities failing, he took to hair shirts and
whips, and the brethren supposed that they had a growing

saint among them. To himself these resources availed
nothing. The temper which he hoped to drive out of
himself clung to him in spite of all prescribed remedies.
But still he persevered ; the novitiate ended, and he took
the vows and became full monk and priest. His father
attended the ceremony, though in no pleasant humour.
' You learned men,' he said at the convent dinner, ' have
you never read that a man should obey his father and
mother ? ' They told him his son had received a call
from Heaven. ' Pray God,' the old man answered, ' it
be not a trick of the devil. I must eat and drink with
you, but I would gladly be gone.'

Two years passed away. Luther occupied himself
with eagerly studying the Bible, but his reading would
not pacify his restless conscientiousness. The Vicar-
General of the Order, Father Staupitz, a wise open-
minded man, saw him, heard his confessions, and understood them. He perceived that his mind was preying
upon itself, and that he required to be taken out of
himself by active employment.

The Elector Frederick—Frederick the Wise, as distinguished from his brother and his nephew—had lately
founded a university at Wittenberg, a considerable town
on the Elbe. The Augustinians had an affiliated house
in Wittenberg, and Staupitz transferred Luther thither,
to teach theology and philosophy.

Luther was now twenty-five, and there is a gap of
two years in his history. He must have observed and
thought much in these years, or the tinder would scarcely
have been kindled by the sparks which fell upon it at
the end of them. The air of Germany was growing thick
with symptoms of storm. After long sleep men were
beginning to think for themselves, and electric flashes

were playing about—sheet lightning still, but strange
and menacing. Religion as it professed to be, and religion as it was embodied in the lives of Church digni-
taries and priests and friars, were in startling contrast,
and the silence with which the difference had been long
observed was being broken by malicious mockeries in the
' Epistolæ Obscurorum Virorum.'

In 1511, business of the Augustinian Order requiring
that two of the brethren from the Electorate should be
sent to Rome, Luther was chosen, with another monk,
for the commission. There were no carriages in those
days, or at least none for humble monks. He walked,
and was six weeks upon the journey, being fed and
lodged at religious houses upon the way. He went full
of hope that in Rome at least, in the heart of Christendom,
and under the eye of the vicegerent of Christ, he would
find the living faith, which far off had grown cold and
mildewed. When he came in sight of the sacred city,
consecrated as it had been by the blood of saints and
martyrs, he flung himself on his knees in a burst of
emotion. His emotion made him exaggerate his disappointment. He found a splendid city, a splendid Court,
good outward order, and careful political administration.
He found art on its highest pinnacle of glory. But it
was Pagan Rome, not Christian. The talk of society
was of Alexander the Sixth and the Borgian infamies.
Julius, the reigning Pontiff, was just returning from the
Venetian wars, where he had led a storming party in
person into the breach of a besieged city. The morals of
the Cardinals were a public jest. Luther himself heard
an officiating priest at the altar say scornfully, ' Bread
thou art, and bread thou remainest.' The very name
' Christian ' was a synonym of a fool. He was perhaps

an imperfect judge of what he observed, and he remained in the city only a month. But the impression left upon him was indelible. 'I would not,' he said afterwards, 'for a hundred thousand gulden have missed the sight of Rome. I might have thought else, that I did the Pope injustice.'

He returned to Wittenberg convinced probably that Popes and Cardinals were no indispensable parts of the Church of Christ, but still with nothing of the spirit of a rebel in him, and he flung himself into his work with enthusiasm. His sermons became famous. He preached with an energy of conviction upon sin and atonement; on human worthlessness, and the mercy and grace of the Almighty; his impassioned words drawn fresh, through his own heart, from the Epistles of St. Paul. His look, his manner, his 'demonic eyes,' brilliant black with a yellow rim round the iris like a lion's, were startling and impressive. People said 'this monk had strange ideas.' The Elector heard him once and took notice. The Elector's chaplain and secretary, Spalatin, became his intimate friend.

The incidents of his life are all related with clear brevity by Herr Köstlin. In this article I must confine myself to the critical epochs. From 1512 to 1517 he remained busy at Wittenberg, little dreaming that he was to be the leader of a spiritual revolution. It was enough for him if he could walk uprightly along the line of his own private duty. The impulse with him, as with all great men, came from without.

Pope Julius was gone. Leo the Tenth succeeded him; and the cultivated Pontiff desired to signalise his reign by building the grandest church in the world. Money was needed, and he opened his spiritual treasury.

He had no belief himself in the specific value of his treasures; but others had, and were willing to pay for them. 'Christianity,' he observed, 'was a profitable fable.' His subjects throughout the world were daily committing sins which involved penance before they could be pardoned. Penances in this life were rarely adequate, and had to be compensated by indefinite ages of purgatory. Purgatory was an unpleasant prospect. The Pope had at his disposal the superfluous merits of extraordinary saints, which could be applied to the payment of the average sinners' debts, if the average sinners chose to purchase them; and commissioners were appointed for a general sale of Indulgences (as they were called) throughout Catholic Europe. The commissioner for Germany was Albert, Archbishop of Mayence, Cardinal and Prince of the Empire, a youth of twenty-seven, a patron of the fine arts like his Holiness—loose, luxurious, and sensual—a rather worse specimen than usual of the average great Churchmen of the age. Köstlin gives a picture of him, a thick-lipped heavy face, with dull eyes, a long drooping nose, and the corners of the mouth turned contemptuously up. The Pope had made him pay lavishly for the pallium when he was admitted to the archbishopric. He had borrowed 30,000 gulden from the Fuggers at Augsburg, the Rothschilds of the sixteenth century. Leo in return had granted him the contract for the Indulgences on favourable terms. The Cardinal was to collect the money; half of it was to be remitted to Rome; half was to go to the repayment of the loan.

It was a business transaction, conducted with the most innocent frankness. Cardinal Albert could not wholly be relied upon. An agent of the Fuggers accompanied each of the sub-commissioners, who carried round the wares, to receive their share of the profit.

A Dominican monk named Tetzel was appointed to collect in Saxony, and he was as accomplished as a modern auctioneer. He entered the towns in procession, companies of priests bearing candles and banners, choristers chanting and ringing bells. At the churches a red cross was set upon the altars, a silk banner floating from it with the Papal arms, and a great iron dish at the foot to receive the equivalents for the myriads of years of the penal fire of Tartarus. Eloquent preachers invited all offenders, the worst especially, robbers, murderers, and adulterers, to avail themselves of the opportunity : insisted on the efficacy of the remedy ; and threatened with excommunication any wretch who dared to question it.

In a world where printed books were beginning to circulate, in a generation which had been reading Erasmus and the ' Epistolæ Obscurorum Virorum,' this proceeding was a high flight of insolence. Superstition had ceased to be a delusion, and had passed into conscious hypocrisy. The Elector Frederick remonstrated. Among the laity there was a general murmur of scorn or anger ; Luther wrote privately to several bishops to entreat their interference ; but none would move, and Tetzel was coming near to Wittenberg. Luther determined to force the question before public opinion. It was common in universities, when there were points unsettled in morals or theology, for any member who pleased to set up propositions for open disputation, to propound an opinion, and offer to maintain it against all comers. The challenger did not commit himself to the adoption of the opinion in his own person. He undertook to defend it in argument, that the opposite side might be heard.

Availing himself of the ordinary practice, on October 31, 1517, the most memorable day in modern European history, Luther, being then thirty-four years old, fixed ninety-five theses on the door of Wittenberg church, calling in question the Papal theory of Indulgences, and the Pope's right to sell them. In itself there was nothing unusual in such a step. No council of the Church had defined or ratified the doctrine of Indulgences. The subject was matter of general conversation, and if the sale of Indulgences could be defended, an opportunity was made for setting uneasy minds at rest. The question, however, was one which could not be set at rest. In a fortnight the theses were flying everywhere, translated into vernacular German. Tetzel condescended only to answer that the Pope was infallible. John Eck, a professor at Ingolstadt, to whom Luther had sent a copy in expectation of sympathy, thundered against him as a Hussite and a heretic. Louder and louder the controversy raged. The witches' caldron had boiled, and the foul lees of popular superstition and priestly abuses came rushing to the surface. Luther himself was frightened at the storm which he had raised. He wrote humbly to Pope Leo, trusting his cause in his hands. Leo was at first amused : ' Brother Martin,' he said, ' has a fair wit ; it is only a quarrel of envious monks.' When the theses were in his hands, and he saw that the matter was serious, he said more impatiently : ' A drunken German has written them—when he is sober he will be of another mind.' But the agitation only grew the wilder. Almost a year passed, and Leo found that he must despatch a Legate (Cardinal Caietanus) into Germany to quiet matters. Along with him he sent an anxious letter to the Emperor Maximilian, with another to the Elector requiring him to deliver 'the child of iniquity' into the Legate's hands, and threatening an interdict if he was disobeyed. A Diet of the Empire was summoned to meet at Augsburg, in August. 1518. Caietanus was present, and Luther was required to attend.

The Elector Frederick was a prudent experienced prince, who had no desire to quarrel with the See of Rome; but he had seen into the infamy of the Indulgences, and did not mean to hand over one of his subjects to the summary process with which the Pope would have closed the controversy. The old Emperor Maximilian was a wise man too. He was German to the heart, and the Germans had no love for Italian supremacy. Pregnant sayings are reported by Luther of Maximilian: ' There are three kings in Europe,' he once observed, 'the Emperor, the King of France, and the King of England. I am a king of kings. If I give an order to the princes of the empire, they obey if they please; if they do not please, they disobey. The King of France is a king of asses. He orders what he pleases, and they obey like asses. The King of England is king of a loyal nation. They obey him with heart and mind as faithful subjects.'

A secretary had embezzled 3,000 gulden. Maximilian sent for him, and asked what should be done to a confidential servant who had robbed his master. The secretary recommended the gallows. ' Nay, nay,' the Emperor said, and tapped him on the shoulder, ' I cannot spare you yet.'

Luther was told that he must appear. He looked for nothing but death, and he thought of the shame which he would bring upon his parents. He had to walk from Wittenberg, and he had no money. At Nuremberg he

borrowed a coat of a friend that he might present himself
in such high company with decency. He arrived at
Augsburg on the 7th of October. The Legate would
have seized him at once; but Maximilian had sent a safe-
conduct for him, and Germany was not prepared to allow
a second treachery like that which had sent Huss to the
stake. The princes of the Diet were out of humour too,
for Caietanus had been demanding money from them, and
they had replied with a list of grievances—complaints of
Annates, first fruits, and Provisions, familiar to the
students of English Reformation history. The Legate
saw that he must temporise with the troublesome monk.
Luther was told that if he would retract he would be
recommended to the Pope, and might look for high
promotion. Caietanus himself then sent for him. Had
the Cardinal been moderate, Luther said afterwards that
he was prepared to yield in much. He was still young,
and diffident, and modest : and it was a great thing for a
peasant's son to stand alone against the ruling powers.
But the Legate was scornful. He could not realise that
this insignificant object before him was a spark of living
fire, which might set the world blazing. He told Luther
briefly that he must retract his theses. Luther said he
could not without some answer to them. Caietan would
not hear of argument. 'Think you,' he said, 'that the
Pope cares for the opinions of Germany? Think you
that the princes will take up arms for you? No indeed.
And where will you be then?' 'Under Heaven,' Luther
answered. He wrote to the Legate afterwards that perhaps he had been too violent. If the sale of Indulgences
was stopped he promised to be silent. Caietan replied
only with a scheme for laying hold on him in spite of his
safe-conduct. Being warned of his danger, he escaped

at night through a postern, and rode off with a guide,
' in a monk's gown and unbreeched,' home to Wittenberg.

The Legate wrote fiercely to the Elector. Luther
offered to leave Saxony and seek an asylum in Paris.
But Frederick replied that the monk had done right in
refusing to retract till the theses had been argued. He
was uneasy; he was no theologian; but he had a sound
instinct that the Indulgences were no better than scan-
dalous robbery. Luther for the present should remain
where he was.

Luther did remain, and was not idle. He published
an account of his interview with the Legate. He wrote
a tract on the Papal supremacy and appealed to a general
council. The Pope found that he must still negotiate.
He had for a chamberlain a Saxon noble, Karl von
Miltitz, a born subject of the Elector. He sent Miltitz
to Frederick with ' the Golden Rose,' the highest com-
pliment which the Court of Rome could pay, with the
politest of letters. He had heard with surprise, he said,
that a child of perdition was preaching heresy in his
dominions. He had the utmost confidence that his
beloved son and the magistrates of the electorate would
put this offspring of Satan to silence. Miltitz arrived in
the middle of the winter 1518–19. He discovered, to his
astonishment, that three-fourths of Germany was on
Luther's side. So fast the flame had spread, that an
army of 25,000 men would not be able to carry him off
by force. He sought an interview with Luther, at which
Spalatin, the Elector's chaplain, was present. He sobbed
and implored; kisses, tears—crocodile's tears—were tried
in profusion. Luther was ready to submit his case to a
synod of German bishops, and wrote again respectfully to
the Pope declining to retract, but hoping that the Holy

See would no longer persist in a course which was creating scandal through Germany.

Perhaps if Maximilian had lived, the Pope would have seen his way to some concession, for Maximilian, it was certain, would never sanction violent courses ; but, in January 1519, Maximilian died, and Charles the Fifth succeeded him. Charles was then but twenty years old ; the Elector Frederick's influence had turned the scale in favour of Maximilian's grandson. There were hopes then that a young prince, coming fresh to the throne in the bitter throes of a new era, might set himself at the head of a national German reformation, and regrets since have been wasted on the disappointment. Regrets for 'what might have been' are proverbially idle. Great movements which are unresisted flow violently on, and waste themselves in extravagance and destruction ; and revolutions which are to mark a step in the advance of mankind need always the discipline of opposition, till the baser parts are beaten out of them. Like the two horses which in Plato's fable draw the chariot of the soul through the vaults of heaven, two principles work side by side in evolving the progress of humanity—the principle of liberty and the principle of authority. Liberty unchecked rushes into anarchy and licence ; authority, if it has no antagonism to fear, stagnates into torpor, or degenerates into tyranny. Luther represented the new life which was beginning ; Charles the Fifth represented the institutions of 1500 years, which, if corrupt in some parts of Europe, in others had not lost their old vitality, and were bearing fruit still in brave and noble forms of human nature. Charles was Emperor of the Germany of Luther, but he was also the King of the Spain of Saint Ignatius. The Spaniards were as earnestly and piously Catholic, as the Germans were about to become Evangelical. Charles was in his religion Spanish. Simple, brave, devout, unaffected, and wise beyond his years, he believed in the faith which he had inherited. Some minds are so constructed as to fly eagerly after new ideas, and the latest born appears the truest; other minds look on speculative novelties as the ephemeral productions of vanity or restlessness, and hold to the creeds which have been tested by experience, and to the profession in which their fathers have lived and died. Both of these modes of thought are good and honourable in themselves, both are essential to the development of truth; yet they rarely coexist in any single person. By nature and instinct Charles the Fifth belonged to the side of authority; and interest, and indeed necessity, combined to hold him to it. In Germany he was king of kings, but of kings over whom, unless he was supported by the Diet, his authority was a shadow. In Spain he was absolute sovereign; and if he had gone with the Reformers against the Pope, he would have lost the hearts of his hereditary subjects. Luther was not to find a friend in Charles; but he was to find a noble enemy, whose lofty qualities he always honoured and admired.

After the failure of Miltitz, the princes of the empire had to decide upon their course. In the summer of 1519 there was an intellectual tournament at Leipzig before Duke George of Saxony. Luther was the champion on one side, John Eck, of Ingolstadt, on the other. We have a description of Luther by a friend who saw him on this occasion: he was of middle height, so lean from study and anxiety that his bones could be counted. He had vast knowledge, command of Scripture, fair acquaintance with Greek and Hebrew; his manner was good; his speech pregnant with matter; in society he was lively, pleasant, and amusing. On his feet, he stood remarkably firm, body bent rather back than forward, the face thrown up, and the eyes flashing like a lion's.

Eck was less favourably drawn : with a face like a butcher's, and a voice like a town crier's; a hesitation in speech which provoked a play upon his name, as being like the *eck, eck, eck* of a jackdaw. Eck called Luther a disciple of John Huss; and Luther defended Huss. Luther had appealed to a general council. Eck reminded him that the Council of Constance had condemned Huss, and so forced him to say that councils might make mistakes. Papal supremacy was next fought over. Did Christ found it? Could it be proved from the New Testament? Duke George thought Eck had the best of the encounter. Leipzig Catholic gossip had a story that Luther's mother had confessed that Martin's father had been the devil. But Luther remained the favourite of Germany. His tracts circulated in hundreds of thousands. Ulrich von Hutten and Franz von Sickingen offered him an asylum if he had to leave the electorate. He published an address to the German nation, denouncing the Papacy as a usurpation, which rang like the blast of a trumpet. He sent a copy to the Elector, who replied with a basket of game.

Eck, meanwhile, who thought the victory had been his, was despatched by Duke George to Rome, to urge the Pope to action. Charles had signified his own intended attitude by ordering Luther's writings to be burnt in the Low Countries. Pope Leo thus encouraged, on the 16th of June, 1520, issued his famous Bull, against ' the wild boar who had broken into the Lord's vineyard.'

Forty-one of Luther's propositions were selected and specially condemned; and Eck was sent back with it to Germany, with orders, if the wild boar was still impenitent, to call in the secular arm. Erasmus, who had been watching the storm from a distance, ill contented, but not without clear knowledge where the right lay, sent word that no good was to be looked for from the young Emperor. Luther, who had made up his mind to death as the immediate outlook for him, was perfectly fearless. The Pope could but kill his body, and he cared only for his soul and for the truth. The Pope had now condemned formally what Luther conceived to be written in the plainest words in Scripture. The Papal chair, therefore, was 'Satan's seat,' and the occupant of it was plainly Antichrist. At the Elector's request he wrote to Leo once more, but he told him, in not conciliatory language, that the See of Rome was worse than Sodom and Gomorrah. When Eck arrived in December, on his commission, Luther ventured the last step, from which there could be no retreat. The Pope had condemned Luther's writings to the fire. On the 10th of December, Luther solemnly burnt at Wittenberg a copy of the Papal Decretals. 'Because,' he said, 'thou hast troubled the Lord's saints, let eternal fire consume thee.' The students of the university sang the Te Deum round the pile, and completed the sacrifice by flinging into the flames the Bull which had been brought by Eck. Luther trembled, he said, before the daring deed was accomplished, but when it was done he was better pleased than with any act of his life. A storm had now burst, he said, which would not end till the day of judgment.

The prophecy was true in a sense deeper than Luther intended. The intellectual conflict which is still raging is the yet uncompleted outcome of that defiance of established authority. Far and wide the news flew. Pamphlets, poems, satires, showered from the printing-presses. As in the dawn of Christianity, house was set against house, and fathers against their sons and daughters. At Rome the frightened courtiers told each other that the monk of Wittenberg was coming with 70,000 barbarians to sack the Holy City, like another Attila.

The Pope replied by excommunicating Luther and all his adherents, and laying the country which harboured him under the threatened interdict. The Elector gave no sign; all eyes were looking to the young Emperor. An Imperial Diet was called, to meet at Worms in 1521, at which Charles was to be present in person, and there Luther was to come and answer for himself. The Elector remembered the fate of John Huss at Constance. Charles might undertake for Luther's safety; but a safe-conduct had not saved Huss, and Popes could dispense with promises. Luther himself had little hope, but also no fear. ' I will go,' he said, ' if I am to be carried sick in my bed. I am called of the Lord when the Kaiser calls me. I trust only that the Emperor of Germany will not begin his reign with shedding innocent blood. I would rather be murdered by the Romans.'

The Diet met on the 21st of January. The princes assembled. The young Emperor came for the first time face to face with them, with a fixed purpose to support the insulted majesty of the spiritual sovereign of Christendom. His first demand was that Luther should be arrested at Wittenberg, and that his patrons should be declared traitors. Seven days followed of sharp debate. The Elector Frederick dared to say that ' he found nothing in the Creed about the Roman Church, but only the Catholic

Christian Church.' 'This monk makes work,' said another; 'some of us would crucify him, and I think he
will hardly escape; but what if he rises again the third
day?' The princes of the empire naturally enough did
not like rebels against lawful authority; but the Elector
was resolute, and it was decided that Luther should not
be condemned without a hearing. The Pope as such had
few friends among them—even Duke George himself insisted that many things needed mending.

Kaspar Sturm, the Imperial herald, was sent to Wittenberg to command Luther's attendance, under pain of
being declared a heretic. The Emperor granted a safe-
conduct, and twenty-one days were allowed. On the 2nd
of April, the Tuesday after Easter, Luther set out on his
momentous journey. He travelled in a cart with three
of his friends, the herald riding in front in his coat of
arms. If he had been anxious about his fate he would
have avoided displays upon the road, which would be
construed into defiance. But Luther let things take their
chance, as if it had been a mere ordinary occasion. The
Emperor had not waited for his appearance to order his
books to be burnt. When he reached Erfurt on the way,
the sentence had just been proclaimed. The herald asked
him if he still meant to go on. 'I will go,' he said, 'if
there are as many devils in Worms as there are tiles upon
the house-tops. Though they burnt Huss, they could not
burn the truth.' The Erfurt students, in retaliation, had
thrown the Bull into the water. The Rector and the
heads of the university gave Luther a formal reception
as an old and honoured member; he preached at his old
convent, and he preached again at Gotha and at Eisenach.
Caietan had protested against the appearance in the Diet
of an excommunicated heretic. The Pope himself had

desired that the safe-conduct should not be respected, and the bishops had said that it was unnecessary. Manœuvres were used to delay him on the road till the time allowed had expired. But there was a fierce sense of fairness in the lay members of the Diet, which it was dangerous to outrage. Franz von Sickingen hinted that if there was foul play it might go hard with Cardinal Caietan—and Von Sickingen was a man of his word in such matters. On the 16th of April, at ten in the morning, the cart entered Worms, bringing Luther in his monk's dress, followed and attended by a crowd of cavaliers. The town's people were all out to see the person with whose name Germany was ringing. As the cart passed through the gates the warder on the walls blew a blast upon his trumpet. The Elector had provided a residence. As he alighted, one who bore him no good will noted the 'demonic eyes' with which he glanced about him. That evening a few nobles called to see him who had been loud in their complaints of Churchmen's exactions at the Diet. Of the princes, one only came, an ardent noble-minded youth, of small influence as yet, but of high-spirited purpose, Philip, Landgrave of Hesse. Instinct, more than knowledge, drew him to Luther's side. 'Dear Doctor,' he said, 'if you are right, the Lord God stand by you.'

Luther needed God to stand by him, for in all that great gathering he could count on few assured friends. The princes of the empire were resolved that he should have fair play, but they were little inclined to favour further a disturber of the public peace. The Diet sate in the Bishop's palace, and the next evening Luther appeared. The presence in which he found himself would have tried the nerves of the bravest of men : the Emperor, sternly hostile, with his retinue of Spanish priests and nobles; the archbishops and bishops, all of opinion that the stake was the only fitting place for so insolent a heretic; the dukes and barons, whose stern eyes were little likely to reveal their sympathy, if sympathy any of them felt. One of them only, George of Frundsberg, had touched Luther on the shoulder as he passed through the ante-room. 'Little monk, little monk,' he said, 'thou hast work' before thee, that I, and many a man whose trade is war, never faced the like of. If thy heart is right, and thy cause good, go on in God's name. He will not forsake thee.'

A pile of books stood on a table when he was brought forward. An officer of the court read the titles, asked if he acknowledged them, and whether he was ready to retract them.

Luther was nervous, not without cause. He answered in a low voice that the books were his. To the other question he could not reply at once. He demanded time. His first appearance had not left a favourable impression; he was allowed a night to consider.

The next morning, April 18, he had recovered himself; he came in fresh, courageous, and collected. His old enemy, Eck, was this time the spokesman against him, and asked what he was prepared to do.

He said firmly that his writings were of three kinds : some on simple Gospel truth, which all admitted, and which of course he could not retract ; some against Papal laws and customs, which had tried the consciences of Christians and had been used as excuses to oppress and spoil the German people. If he retracted these he would cover himself with shame. In a third sort he had attacked particular persons, and perhaps had been too violent.

Even here he declined to retract simply, but would admit his fault if fault could be proved.

He gave his answers in a clear strong voice, in Latin first, and then in German. There was a pause, and then Eck said that he had spoken disrespectfully; his heresies had been already condemned at the Council at Constance; let him retract on these special points, and he should have consideration for the rest. He required a plain Yes or No from him, 'without horns.' The taunt roused Luther's blood. His full brave self was in his reply. 'I will give you an answer,' he said, 'which has neither horns nor teeth. Popes have erred and councils have erred. Prove to me out of Scripture that I am wrong, and I submit. Till then my conscience binds me. Here I stand. I can do no more. God help me. Amen.'

All day long the storm raged. Night had fallen, and torches were lighted in the hall before the sitting closed. Luther was dismissed at last; it was supposed, and perhaps intended, that he was to be taken to a dungeon. But the hearts of the lay members of the Diet had been touched by the courage which he had shown. They would not permit a hand to be laid on him. Duke Eric of Brunswick handed to him a tankard of beer which he had himself half drained. When he had reached his lodging again, he flung up his hands. 'I am through!' he cried, 'I am through! If I had a thousand heads, they should be struck off one by one before I would retract.' The same evening the Elector Frederick sent for him, and told him he had done well and bravely.

But though he had escaped so far, he was not acquitted. Charles conceived that he could be now dealt with as an obstinate heretic. At the next session (the day following), he informed the Diet that he would send

Luther home to Wittenberg, there to be punished as the
Church required. The utmost that his friends could
obtain was that further efforts should be made. The
Archbishop of Treves was allowed to tell him that if he
would acknowledge the infallibility of councils, he might
be permitted to doubt the infallibility of the Pope. But
Luther stood simply upon Scripture. There, and there
only, was infallibility. The Elector ordered him home at
once, till the Diet should decide upon his fate ; and he was
directed to be silent on the way, with significant reference
to his Erfurt sermon. A majority in the Diet, it was
now clear, would pronounce for his death. If he was
sentenced by the Great Council of the Empire, the Elector
would be no longer able openly to protect him. It was
decided that he should disappear, and disappear so completely that no trace of him should be discernible. On
his way back through the Thuringian Forest, three or
four miles from Altenstein, a party of armed men started
out of the wood, set upon his carriage, seized and carried
him off to Wartburg Castle. There he remained, passing
by the name of the Ritter George, and supposed to be
some captive knight. The secret was so well kept, that
even the Elector's brother was ignorant of his hiding-
place. Luther was as completely lost as if the earth had
swallowed him. Some said that he was with Von Sickingen ; others that he had been murdered. Authentic
tidings of him there were none. On the 8th of May the
Edict of Worms was issued, placing him under the ban
of the empire ; but he had become ' as the air invul-
nerable,' and the face of the world had changed before
he came back to it.

The appearance of Luther before the Diet on this
occasion is one of the finest, perhaps it is the very finest,

scene in human history. Many a man has encountered death bravely for a cause which he knows to be just, when he is sustained by the sympathy of thousands, of whom he is at the moment the champion and the representative. But it is one thing to suffer and another to encounter face to face and single-handed the array of spiritual and temporal authorities which are ruling supreme. Luther's very cause was yet unshaped and undetermined, and the minds of those who had admired and followed him were hanging in suspense for the issue of his trial. High-placed men of noble birth are sustained by pride of blood and ancestry, and the sense that they are the equals of those whom they defy. At Worms there was on one side a solitary low-born peasant monk, and on the other the Legate of the dreaded power which had broken the spirit of Kings and Emperors—sustained and personally supported by the Imperial Majesty itself and the assembled princes of Germany before whom the poor peasantry had been taught to tremble as beings of another nature from themselves. Well might George of Frundsberg say that no knight among them all had ever faced a peril which could equal this.

The victory was won. The wavering hearts took courage. The Evangelical revolt spread like an epidemic. The Papacy was like an idol, powerful only as long as it was feared. Luther had thrown his spear at it, and the enchantment was broken. The idol was but painted wood, which men and boys might now mock and jibe at. Never again had Charles another chance of crushing the Reformation. France fell out with him on one side, and for the rest of his life gave him but brief intervals of breathing time. The Turks hung over Austria like a thunder cloud, terrified Ferdinand in Vienna, and swarmed over the Mediterranean in their pirate galleys. Charles was an earnest Catholic; but he was a statesman also, too wise to add to his difficulties by making war on heresy. What some call Providence and others accident had so ordered Europe that the tree which Luther had planted was allowed to grow till it was too strongly rooted to be overthrown.

Luther's abduction and residence at Wartburg is the most picturesque incident in his life. He dropped his monk's gown, and was dressed like a gentleman; he let his beard grow and wore a sword. In the castle he was treated as a distinguished guest. Within the walls he was free to go where he liked. He rode in the forest with an attendant, and as the summer came on, walked about and gathered strawberries. In August there was a two days' hunt, at which, as Ritter George, he attended, and made his reflections on it. 'We caught a few hares and partridges,' he said, 'a worthy occupation for idle people.' In the 'nets and dogs' he saw the devil entangling or pursuing human souls. A hunted hare ran to his feet; he sheltered it for a moment, but the hounds tore it in pieces. 'So,' he said, 'rages the Pope and Satan to destroy those whom I would save.' The devil, he believed, haunted his own rooms. That he threw his ink-bottle at the devil is unauthentic; but there were noises in his boxes and closets which, he never doubted, came from his great enemy. When he heard the sounds, he made jokes at them, and they ceased. 'The devil,' he said, 'will bear anything better than to be laughed at.'

The revolution, deprived of its leader, ran wild meanwhile. An account of the scene at Worms, with Luther's speeches, and woodcut illustrations, was printed on broadsheets and circulated in hundreds of thousands of copies. The people were like schoolboys left without a master. Convents and monasteries dissolved by themselves; monks and nuns began to marry; there was nothing else for the nuns to do, turned, as they were, adrift without provision. The Mass in most of the churches in Saxony was changed into a Communion. But without Luther it was all chaos, and no order could be taken. So great was the need of him, that in December he went to Wittenberg in disguise; but it was not yet safe for him to remain there. He had to retreat to his castle again, and in that compelled retreat he bestowed on Germany the greatest of all the gifts which he was able to offer. He began to translate the Bible into clear vernacular German. The Bible to him was the sole infallible authority, where every Christian for himself could find the truth and the road to salvation, if he faithfully and piously looked for it. He had probably commenced the work at the beginning of his stay at the castle. In the spring of 1522 the New Testament was completed. In the middle of March the Emperor's hands now being fully occupied, the Elector sent him word that he need not conceal himself any longer; and he returned finally to his home and his friends.

The New Testament was printed in November of that year, and became at once a household book in Germany. The contrast visible to the simplest eyes between the tawdry splendid Papacy and Christ and the Apostles, settled for ever the determination of the German people to have done with the old idolatry. The Old Testament was taken in hand at once, and in two years half of it was roughly finished. Luther himself, confident now that a special Providence was with him, showered out

controversial pamphlets not caring any longer to measure
his words. Adrian VI., Clement VII., clamoured for
the execution of the Edict of Worms. The Emperor,
from a distance, denounced the new Mahomet. But they
spoke to deaf ears. The Diet answered only with lists
of grievances, and a demand for a free Council, to be held
in Germany itself.

The Reformation had risen out of the people; and it
is the nature of popular movements, when the bonds of
authority are once broken, to burst into anarchy. Luther
no longer believed in an apostolically ordained priesthood; but he retained a pious awe for the sacraments,
which he regarded really and truly as mysterious sources
of grace. Zwingle in Switzerland, Carlstadt and others
in Saxony, looked on the sacraments as remnants of
idolatrous superstition. Carlstadt himself, 'Archdeacon
of Orlamund,' as he was called, had sprung before his
age into notions of universal equality and brotherhood.
Luther found him one day metamorphosed into 'Neigh-
bour Andrew,' on a dungheap loading a cart. A more
dangerous fanatic was Münzer, the parson of Allstadt,
near Weimar. It was not the Church only which needed
reform. The nobles had taken to luxury and amusement.
Toll and tax lay heavy on their peasant tenants; as the
life in the castle had grown splendid, the life in the cabin
had become hard and bitter. Luther had confined himself to spiritual matters, but the spiritual and the secular
were too closely bound together to be separated. The
Allstadt parson, after much 'conversing with God,' discovered that he had a mission to establish the Kingdom
of the Saints, where tyrants were to be killed, and all men
were to live as brothers, and all property was to be in
common. Property, like all else which man may possess,

is a trust which he holds, not for his own indulgence, but for the general good. This is a universal principle. Nature is satisfied with a very imperfect recognition of it; but if there is no recognition, if the upper classes, as they are called, live only for pleasure, and only for them. selves, the conditions are broken under which human beings can live together, and society rushes into chaos. The rising spread, 1524–25. The demands actually set forward fell short of the Anabaptist ideal, and were not in themselves unreasonable. The people required to be allowed to choose their own pastors, an equitable adjustment of tithes, emancipation from serfdom, and lastly, liberty to kill game—a right for a poor man to feed his starving children with a stray hare or rabbit. Luther saw nothing in this petition which might not be wisely conceded. But Münzer himself made concession impossible. He raised an 'Army of the Lord.' He marched through the country, burning castles and convents, towns and villages, and executing savage vengeance on the persons of the 'Lord's enemies.' It was the heaviest blow which Luther had received. His enemies could say, and say with a certain truth, 'Here was the visible fruit of his own action.' He knew that he was partly responsible, and that without him these scenes would not have been. The Elector, unfortunately, was ill—mortally so. He died while the insurrection was still blazing. His brother John succeeded, very like him in purpose and character, and proceeded instantly to deal with the emergency. Luther hurried up and down the country, preaching to the people, rebuking the tyrannous Counts and Barons, and urging the Protestant Princes to exert themselves to keep the peace. Philip of Hesse, the Duke of Brunswick, and Count Mansfelt collected a force.

The peasants were defeated and scattered. Münzer was taken and hanged, and the fire was extinguished. It was well for Luther that the troops which had been employed were exclusively Protestant. The Catholics said scornfully of him, ' He kindled the flame, and he washes his hands like Pilate.' Had the army raised to quell the peasants belonged to Ferdinand, the Edict of Worms would have been made a reality.

The Landgrave and the new Elector, John, allowed no severe retaliation when armed resistance was over. They set themselves to cure, as far as possible, the causes of discontent. They trusted, as Luther did, to the return of a better order of things from 'a revival of religion.'

The Peasant War had been the first scandal to the Reformation. The second, which created scarcely less disturbance, was Luther's own immediate work. As a priest he had taken a vow of celibacy. As a monk he had again bound himself by a vow of chastity.

In priesthood and monkery he had ceased to believe. If the orders themselves were unreal, the vows to respect the rules of those orders might fairly be held to be nugatory. Luther not only held that the clergy, as a rule, might be married, but he thought it far better that they should be married; and the poor men and women who were turned adrift on the breaking up of the religious houses he had freely advised to marry without fear or scruple. But still around a vow a certain imagined sanctity persisted in adhering; and when he was recommended to set an example to others who were hesitating, he considered, and his friend, Melanchthon, considered, that, in his position, and with so many indignant eyes turned upon him, he ought not to give occasion to the enemy. Once, indeed, impatiently, he said that marry he would, to spite the devil. But he had scarcely a home to offer to any woman, and no leisure and no certainty of companionship. He was for some years after the Edict of Worms in constant expectation of being executed as a heretic. He still lived in the Augustinian convent at Wittenberg; but the monks had gone, and there were no revenues. He had no income of his own; one suit of clothes served him for two years; the Elector at the end of them gave him a piece of cloth for another. The publishers made fortunes out of his writings, but he never received a florin for them. So ill-attended he was that for a whole year his bed was never made, and was mildewed with perspiration. ' I was tired out with each day's work,' he said, ' and lay down and knew no more.'

But things were getting into order again in the Electorate. The parishes were provided with pastors, and the pastors with modest wages. Luther was professor at the university, and the Elector allowed him a salary of 200 gulden a year.[1] Presents came from other quarters, and he began to think that it was not well for him to be alone. In Wittenberg there was a certain Catherine von Bora, sixteen years younger than he, who had been a nun in a distant convent. Her family were noble, but poor; they had provided for their daughter by placing her in the cloister when she was a child of nine; at sixteen she had taken the vows; but she detested the life into which she had been forced, and when the movement began she had applied to her friends to take her out of it. The friends would do nothing; but in April 1523 she and nine others were released by the people. As they were starving, Luther collected money to provide

---

[1] Equal to about 30*l.* of modern money.

for them, and Catherine von Bora, being then twenty-
four years old, came to Wittenberg to reside with the
burgomaster, Philip Reichenbach. Luther did not at
first like her; she was not beautiful, and he thought that
she was proud of her birth and blood; but she was a
simple, sensible, shrewd, active woman; she, in the sense
in which Luther was, might consider herself dedicated to
God, and a fit wife for a religious reformer. Luther's
own father was most anxious that he should marry, and
in a short time they came to understand each other. So
on the 13th of June, 1525, a month after Münzer had
been stamped out at Frankenhausen, a little party was
collected in the Wittenberg Cloister—Bugenhagen, the
town pastor, Professor Jonas, Lucas Cranach (the painter),
with his wife, and Professor Apel, of Bamberg, who had
himself married a nun; and in this presence Martin
Luther and Catherine von Bora became man and wife.
It was a nine days' wonder. Philip Melanchthon thought
his friend was undone; Luther himself was uneasy for a
day or two. But the wonder passed off; in the town
there was hearty satisfaction and congratulation. The
new Elector, John, was not displeased. The conversion
of Germany was not arrested. Prussia and Denmark
broke with Rome and accepted Luther's Catechism. In
1526, at Torgau, the Elector John, the Landgrave, the
Dukes of Brunswick, Lüneberg, Anhalt, Mecklenburg,
and Magdeburg, formed themselves into an Evangelical Confederacy. It was a measure of self-defence,
for it had appeared for the moment as if the Emperor
might again be free for a Papal crusade. The French
had been defeated at Pavia; Francis was a prisoner, and
Christendom was at Charles's feet. But Francis was
soon loose again. In the cross purposes of politics,

France and the Pope became allies, and the Pope was the Emperor's enemy. Rome was stormed by a German-Spanish army; and the Emperor, in spite of himself, was doing Luther's work in breaking the power of the great enemy. Then England came into the fray, with the divorce of Catherine and the assertion of spiritual independence; and the Protestant States were left in peace till calmer times and the meeting of the promised Council. In the midst of the confusion, Luther was able to work calmly on, ordering the churches, appointing visitors, or crossing swords with Erasmus, who looked on Luther much as the Pope did—as a wild boar who had broken into the vineyard. Luther, however violent in his polemics, was leading meanwhile the quietest of lives. He had taken his garden in hand; he had built a fountain; planted fruit trees and roots and seeds. He had a little farm; he bought threshing instruments, and learned to use the flail. If the worst came to the worst he found that he could support his family with his hands.

Again, in 1530, it seemed as if the Emperor would find leisure to interfere. In the year before he had made a peace with the Pope and the French which, for the sake of Christendom and the faith, he hoped might be observed. The Turks had been under the walls of Vienna, but they had retreated with enormous loss, and seemed inclined at least to a truce. The Evangelicals began to consider seriously how far they might go in resistance should Charles attempt to coerce them into obedience. Luther, fiery as he was in the defence of the faith, refused to sanction civil war. A Christian must suffer all extremities rather than deny his God; but he might not fight in the field against his lawful sovereign. In worldly things the ruler was supreme, and the Emperor was the

ruler of Germany. The Emperor, he said, had been
chosen by the Electors, and by their unanimous vote
might be deposed; but he would not encourage either
the Landgrave or his own Elector to meet force by force
in separate action. The question never rose in Luther's
lifetime, but the escape was a near one. A Diet at
Speyer, in 1526, had decided that each prince should
rule his own dominions in his own way, pending the
expected Council. Charles's conscience would not allow
him to tolerate a Lutheran communion if he could pre
vent it; but he, too, dreaded a war of religion, of which
no one could foresee any issue save the ruin of Germany.
He knew and respected Luther's moderation, and summoned the Diet to meet him again at Augsburg, in the
spring of 1530, to discover, if possible, some terms of
reconciliation. The religious order which had been established in Saxony was recognised even at Rome with
agreeable surprise, and the Legate who attended was said
to be prepared with certain concessions. The Elector
John intended to have taken Luther to the Diet with
him, but at Coburg a letter met him from the Emperor,
intimating that Luther, being under the ban of the
empire, could not be admitted into his presence. The
Elector went forward with Melanchthon and Jonas;
Luther stayed behind in Coburg Castle, to work at his
translation of the Bible, and to compare the rooks and
jackdaws, when they woke in the morning, to gatherings
of learned Doctors wrangling over their sophistries.

We have seen him hitherto as a spiritual athlete. We
here catch a glimpse of him in a softer character. His
eldest boy, Hans, had been born four years before. From
Coburg he wrote him perhaps the prettiest letter ever
addressed by a father to a child :—

Grace and peace in Christ, my dear little boy. I am pleased to see that thou learnest thy lessons well, and prayest well. Go on thus, my dear boy, and when I come home I will bring you a fine 'fairing.' I know of a pretty garden, where are merry children that have gold frocks, and gather nice apples and plums and cherries under the trees, and sing and dance, and ride on pretty horses with gold bridles and silver saddles. I asked the man of the place whose the garden was, and who the children were. He said, 'These are the children who pray and learn and are good.' Then I answered, 'I also have a son, who is called Hans Luther. May he come to this garden and eat pears and apples and ride a little horse, and play with the others?' The man said, 'If he says his prayers, and learns, and is good, he may come ; and Lippus and Jost may come,[1] and they shall have pipes and drums and lutes and fiddles, and they shall dance and shoot with little crossbows.' Then he showed me a smooth lawn in the garden laid out for dancing, and there the pipes and drums and crossbows hung. But it was still early and the children had not dined ; and I could not wait for the dance. So I said, 'Dear sir, I will go straight home and write all this to my little boy ; but he has an aunt, Lene,[2] that he must bring with him.' And the man answered, 'So it shall be ; go and write as you say.' Therefore, dear little boy, learn and pray with a good heart, and tell Lippus and Jost to do the same, and then you will all come to the garden together. Almighty God guard you. Give my love to aunt Lene, and give her a kiss for me.—Your loving father, MARTIN LUTHER.

The Emperor meanwhile arrived at Augsburg on the 15th of June. Melanchthon, who was eager for peace, had prepared a Confession of Faith, softening as far as possible the points of difference between the Evangelicals and the Catholics. It was laid before the Diet, and was received

---

[1] Melanchthon's son, Philip, and Jonas's son Jodocus.
[2] Great-aunt, Magdalen.

with more favour than Melanchthon looked for even by
Charles himself.   Melanchthon believed that spiritual
agreement might be possible; Luther knew that it was
impossible; but he did think that a political agreement
might be arrived at; that the two creeds, which in so
many essentials were the same, might be allowed to
live side by side.

'Do not let us fall out,' he wrote to Cardinal Albert.
'Do not let us ruin Germany.   Let there be liberty of
conscience, and let us save our fatherland.'   Melanchthon
was frightened, and would have yielded much.   Luther
would not yield an inch.   When no progress was made,
he advised his friends to leave the Diet and come away.
'Threats do not kill,' he said.   'There will be no war.'

Luther understood the signs of the times.   With the
Turks in Hungary, and Henry VIII. and Francis in
alliance, it was in vain that the Pope urged violent
measures.   The Evangelical Confession was not accepted,
and the Emperor demanded submission.   The Landgrave
replied that if this was to be the way, he would go home
and take measures to defend himself.   Charles, taking
leave of the Elector, said sadly he had expected better of
him; the Elector's eyes filled with tears; but he answered
nothing.   The end, however, was as Luther expected.
Ferdinand of Austria and the Duke of Bavaria agreed to
prohibit the advance of the new doctrines in their own
dominions.   It was decided, on the other hand, among
the Protestant princes, that the Emperor's authority was
limited, that resistance to unconstitutional interference
was not unlawful, an opinion to which Luther himself
unwillingly assented.   The famous League of Schmalkald
was formed for the general defence of spiritual liberty.
Denmark held out a hand from a distance, and France and

England courted an alliance, which would hold Charles in check at home. The Emperor and even Ferdinand, who was the more bigoted of the two brothers, admitted the necessity to which they were compelled to yield. The united strength of Germany was barely sufficient to bear back the Turkish invasion, and the political peace which Luther anticipated was allowed to stand for an indefinite period.

Luther was present at Schmalkald, where he preached to the assembled representatives. On the day of the sermon he became suddenly and dangerously ill. His health had been for some time uncertain. He was subject to violent headaches and giddiness; he was now prostrated by an attack of 'the stone,' so severe that he thought he was dying. He had finished his translation of the Bible. It was now printed: a complete possession which he was able to bequeath to his countrymen. He conceived that his work was done, and life for its own sake had long ceased to have much interest for him. 'At his age,' he said, 'with strength failing, he felt so weary, that he had no will to protract his days any longer in such an accursed world.' At Schmalkald the end seemed to have come. Such remedies as then were known for the disease under which he was suffering were tried. Luther hated doctors; but he submitted to all their prescriptions. His body swelled. 'They made me drink water,' he said, 'as if I was a great ox.' Mechanical contrivances were employed, equally ineffectual, and he prepared to die. 'I depart,' he cried to his Maker, 'a foe of Thy foes, cursed and banned by Thy enemy, the Pope. May he, too, die under Thy ban, and we both stand at Thy judgment bar on that day.' The Elector, the young John Frederick—the Elector John, his father, was by this time gone—stood by his bed, and promised to care for his wife and children. Melanchthon was weeping. Even at that supreme moment Luther could not resist his humour. 'Have we not received good at the hand of the Lord,' he said, ' and shall we not receive evil? The Jews stoned Stephen; my stone, the villain, is stoning me.'

But he had some years of precious life yet waiting for him. He became restless, and insisted on being carried home. He took leave of his friends. ' The Lord fill you with his blessing,' he said, ' and with hatred of the Pope.' The first day he reached Tambach. The movement of the cart tortured him; but it effected for him what the doctors could not. He had been forbidden to touch wine. He drank a goblet notwithstanding. He was relieved, and recovered.

We need not specially concern ourselves with the events of the next few years. They were spent in correcting and giving final form to the translation of the Bible, in organising the churches, in correspondence with the princes, and in discussing the conditions of the long-talked-of Council, and of the terms on which the Evangelicals would consent to take part in it. The peace of Nuremberg seemed an admission that no further efforts would be made to crush the Reformation by violence, and Luther was left to a peaceful, industrious life in his quiet home at Wittenberg. A very beautiful home it was. If Luther's marriage was a scandal, it was a scandal that was singularly happy in its consequences. The house in which he lived, as has been already said, was the old cloister to which he had first been brought from Erfurt. It was a pleasant, roomy building on the banks of the Elbe, and close to the town wall. His wife and he when they married were both penniless, but his salary as professor was raised to 300 gulden, and some small payments in kind were added from the university. The Elector sent him presents. Denmark, the Free Towns, great men from all parts of Europe, paid honour to the Deliverer of Germany with offerings of plate or money. The money, even the plate, too, he gave away, for he was profusely generous; and any fugitive nun or brother suffering for the faith never appealed in vain while Luther had a kreutzer. But in his later years his own modest wants were more than amply supplied. He bought a farm, with a house upon it, where his family lived after his death. Katie, as he called his wife, managed everything; she attended to the farm, she kept many pigs, and doubtless poultry also. She had a fish pond. She brewed beer. She had a strong ruling, administering talent. She was as great in her way as her husband was in his.

'Next to God's Word,' he said, 'the world has no more precious treasure than holy matrimony. God's best gift is a pious, cheerful, God-fearing, home-keeping wife, to whom you can trust your goods, and body, and life. There are couples who neither care for their families, nor love each other. People like these are not human beings. They make their homes a hell.'

The household was considerable. Five children were born in all. Hans, the eldest, to whom the letter from Coburg was written, died early. Elizabeth, the next daughter, died also very young. There were three others, Magdalen, Martin, and Paul. Magdalen von Bora, Katie's aunt, the 'Lene' of the letter from Coburg, lived with the family. She had been a nun in the same convent with her niece. For her Luther had a most affectionate regard. When she was dying, he said to her,

' You will not die ; you will sleep away as in a cradle, and morning will dawn, and you will rise and live for ever.'

Two nieces seem to have formed part of the establishment, and two nephews also. There was a tutor for the boys, and a secretary. A certain number of university students boarded in the house—lads perhaps of promise, in whom Luther had a special interest. To his children he was passionately devoted. He had no sentimental weakness ; but the simple lightheartedness, the unquestioning confidence and trustfulness of children, was in itself peculiarly charming to him. Life when they came to maturity would bring its own sorrows with it. A few bright and happy years to look back upon would be something which could not afterwards be taken away. He refused boys and girls no kind of innocent enjoyment, and in all the anecdotes of his relations with them there is an exquisite tenderness and playfulness. His Katie he was not above teasing and occasionally mocking. She was a ' Martha' more than a ' Mary,' always busy, always managing and directing with an eye to business. He was very fond of her. He never seriously found fault with those worldly ways of hers, for he knew her sterling worth ; but he told her once he would give her fifty gulden if she would read the Bible through. He called her his Herr Katie, and his Gnädige Frau. The farm which he had bought for her was called Zulsdorf. One of his last letters is addressed to ' my heartily beloved housewife, Katherin Lady Luther, Lady Doctor, Lady Zulsdorf, Lady of the Pigmarket, or whatever else she may be.'

The religious education of his children he conducted himself. His daughter Magdalen was an unusually interesting girl. A picture of her remains, by Cranach, with large imaginative eyes. Luther saw in her the pro mise of a beautiful character; she died when she was fourteen, and he was almost heart-broken. When she was carried to her grave he said to the bearers : ‘ I have sent a saint to heaven : could mine be such a death as hers, I would die at this moment.’ To his friend Jonas he wrote :—‘ You will have heard that my dearest child is born again in the eternal kingdom of God. We ought to be glad at her departure, for she is taken away from the world, the flesh, and the devil; but so strong is natural love that we cannot bear it without anguish of heart, without the sense of death in ourselves. When I think of her words, her gestures, when she was with us and in her departing, even Christ’s death cannot relieve my agony.’ On her tomb he wrote these lines : —

> Hier schlaf Ich, Lenchen, Luther’s Töchterlein,
> Ruh’ mit all’n Heiligen in meine Bettlein.
> Die Ich in Sünden war geborn
> Hatt’ ewig müssen seyn verlorn,
> Aber Ich leb nu und habs gut
> Herr Christe erlost mit deinem Blut.

> Here do I Lena, Luther’s daughter rest,
> Sleep in my little bed with all the Blest.
> In sin and trespass was I born,
> For ever was I thus forlorn ; [1]
> But yet I live, and all is good—
> Thou, Christ, redeem’st me with Thy blood.

There is yet another side to Luther, and it is the most wonderful of all. We have seen him as a theologian ; we have seen him standing up alone, before principalities and powers, to protest against spiritual lies ; we have seen him at home in the quiet circle of his household. But

---

[1] *Verloren.*—The word has travelled away from its original meaning.

there is nothing in any of this to show that his thoughts
had travelled beyond the limits of a special set of subjects.
But Luther's mind was literally world-wide ; his eyes were
for ever observant of what was round him.   At a time
when science was scarcely out of its shell, Luther had
observed Nature with the liveliest curiosity.   He had
anticipated by mere genius the generative functions of
flowers.   Human nature he had studied like a dramatist.
His memory was a museum of historical information,
of anecdotes of great men, of old German literature and
songs and proverbs.   Scarce a subject could be spoken of
on which he had not thought, and on which he had not
something remarkable to say.   His table was always
open, and amply furnished.   Melanchthon, Jonas, Lucas
Cranach, and other Wittenberg friends, were constant
guests.   Great people, great lords, great ladies, great
learned men, came from all parts of Europe.   He
received them freely at dinner, and being one of the
most copious of talkers, he enabled his friends to
preserve the most extraordinary monument of his ac-
quirements and of his intellectual vigour.   On reading
the *Tischreden* or Table-talk of Luther, one ceases to
wonder how this single man could change the face of
Europe.

Where the language is itself beautiful, it necessarily
loses in translation ; I will endeavour, however, to con-
vey some notion of Luther's mind as it appears in these
conversations.

First, for his thoughts about Nature.

A tree in his garden was covered with ripe fruit.
' Ah,' he said, ' if Adam had not fallen, we should have
seen the beauty of these things—every bush and shrub
would have seemed more lovely than if it was made of gold

and silver. It is really more lovely ; but since Adam's fall men see nothing, and are stupider than beasts. God's power and wisdom are shown in the smallest flowers. Painters cannot rival their colour, nor perfumers their sweetness ; green and yellow, crimson, blue, and purple, all growing out of the earth. And we do not know how to use them to God's honour. We only misuse them ; and we trample on lilies as if we were so many cows.'

Katie had provided some fish out of her pond. Luther spoke of the breeding of fish, and what an extraordinary thing it was ; he then turned to the breeding of other creatures. 'Look at a pair of birds,' he said. ' They build a neat little nest, and drop their eggs in it, and sit on them. Then come the chicks. There is the creature rolled up inside the shell. If we had never seen such a thing before, and an egg was brought from Calicut, we should be all wondering and crying out. Philosophers cannot explain how the chick is made. God spake, and it was done : He commanded, and so it was. But he acts in all His works rather comically. If He had consulted me, I should have advised Him to make His men out of lumps of clay, and to have set the sun like a lamp, on the earth's surface, that it might be always day.'

Looking at a rose, he said, ' Could a man make a single rose, we should give him an empire ; but these beautiful gifts of God come freely to us, and we think nothing of them. We admire what is worthless, if it be only rare. The most precious of things is nothing if it be common.' In the spring, when the buds were swelling and the flowers opening, he exclaimed : ' Praise be to God the Creator, that now in this time of Lent out

of dead wood makes all alive again. Look at that
bough, as if it was with child and full of young things
coming to the birth. It is a figure of our faith—winter
is death, summer is the resurrection.'

He was sitting one night late out of doors. A bird
flew into a tree to roost. ' That bird,' he said, ' has had
its supper, and will now sleep safe as the bough, and
leave God to care for him. If Adam's fall had not spoilt
us, we should have had no care either. We should have
lived without pain, in possession of all kinds of knowledge, and have passed from time into eternity without
feeling of death.' The old question was asked why God
made man at all if He knew that he would fall? Luther
answered, that a great Lord must have vessels of dis-
honour in his house as well as vessels of honour. There
were fellows who thought when they had heard a sermon
or two, that they knew everything, and had swallowed
the Holy Ghost feathers and all. Such wretches had no
right to criticize the actions of God. Man could not
measure structures of God's building : he saw only the
scaffolding. In the next life he would see it all ; and
then happy those who had resisted temptation.

Little Martin had been busy dressing a doll.

In Paradise (Luther said) we shall be as simple as this
child who talks of God and has no doubts to trouble him.
Natural merriment is the best food for children—and they
are themselves the best of playthings. They speak and act
from the heart. They believe in God without disputing,
and in another life beyond the present. They have small
intellect, but they have faith, and are wiser than old fools
like us. They think of heaven as a place where there will be
eating and dancing, and rivers running with milk. Happy
they ! for they have no earthly cares, or fears of death or
hell. They have only pure thoughts and bright dreams.

Abraham must have had a bad time when he was told to kill Isaac. If God had given me such an order, I should have disputed the point with him.

'I never will believe,' said the downright Katie, 'that God ordered any man to kill his child.'

Luther answered : 'God had nothing dearer to Him than His own Son. Yet He gave Him to be hanged on the cross. In man's judgment He was more like a father to Caiaphas and Pilate than He was to Christ.'

The religious houses were falling all round Germany. Bishops losing their functions were losing their lands ; and the nobles and burghers who had professed the Gospel were clutching at the spoils. Luther could see that ill had come with the change as well as good.

'Look,' he said sadly, 'at the time when the truth was unknown, and men were lost in idolatry, and trusted in their own works. Then was charity without end or measure. Then it snowed with gifts. Cloisters were founded, and there were endowments for Mass priests. Churches were splendidly decorated. How blind is the world become.' Drunkenness, too, seemed to spread, and usury and a thousand other vices. It tried his faith. Yet he said, 'Never do we act better than when we know not what we are doing, or than when we think we are foolish and imprudent, for strength is perfected in weakness, and the best we do is what comes straight from the heart.'

The Protestants were not the only spoilers of the Church lands. Some one told a story of a dog at Lintz, which used to go every day with a basket to the market to fetch meat. One day some other dogs set upon him. He fought for his basket as long as he could ; but when he could fight no longer he snatched a piece of meat for himself and ran away with it. 'There is Kaiser Karl,' said Luther. 'He defended the estates of the Church while it was possible. But when the princes all began to plunder, he seized a few bishoprics as his own share.'

He had a high respect generally for princes and nobles, and had many curious anecdotes of such great persons. He did not think them much to be envied.

'Sovereigns and magistrates,' he said, 'have weighty things to handle, and have a sore time with them. The peasant is happy; he has no cares. He never troubles himself as to how the world is going. If a peasant knew what the prince has to bear, he would thank God that made him what he was. But he sees only the outside splendour, the fine clothes, the gold chains, the castles and palaces. He never dreams of the perils and anxieties that beset great lords while he is stewing his pears at his stove. The Elector Frederick used to say that the peasant's life was the best of all; and that happiness grew less at each step of the scale. The Emperor had most to trouble him, the princes next; the nobles had endless vexations, and the burghers, though better off than the nobles, had their trade losses and other worries. The peasant could watch his crops grow by the grace of God; he sold what was needed to pay his tithes and taxes, and lived in peace and quiet. The servants in a family are easier than their masters. They do their work, and eat and drink and sing. My people, Wolf and Dorothy (the cook), are better off than I and Katie. The higher you stand, the more your danger. Yet no one is content with his position. When the ass is well off, he begins to caper, and breaks his leg.'

He loved and honoured his own Electors, but he thought they were over gentle. 'The Elector Frederick,' he said, 'was unwilling to punish evil doers. "Yes," he would say, "it is easy to take a man's life; but can you give it him back?" The Elector John would say, "Ah! he will be a good fellow yet." God is merciful, but He is also just. Yet Dr. Schurf, one of our best judges, and a Christian man, cannot bear to hang a felon. The proverb says: "A thief for the gallows, a monk for the cloister, and a fish for the water." '

He had a respect for Pilate, and said some curious things about him. Pilate, he declared, was a better man than many Popish princes; he stood by the law, and would not have a prisoner condemned unheard. He tried many ways to release Christ; he yielded at last when he was threatened with Cæsar's anger. 'After all,' thought Pilate, 'it is but one poor wretch, who has no one to take His part; better He should die than the whole people become His enemies.' 'Why,' it was asked, 'did Pilate scourge Christ?' 'Pilate,' Luther said, 'was a man of the world; he scourged Him in the hope that the Jews would then be satisfied.' When he asked Christ what truth was, he meant 'What is the use of speaking truth in such a scene as this? Truth won't help you; look for some trick of law, and so you may escape.' It was asked again what object the devil could have had in moving Pilate's wife to interfere. Luther seemed to admit that it was the devil. 'The devil,' he answered, 'said to himself, I have strangled ever so many prophets and have gained nothing by it; Christ is not afraid of death; better He should live, and I shall perhaps be able to tempt Him to do something wrong. The devil has fine notions in him; he is no fool.'

He had a high opinion of the Landgrave of Hesse, whom he called another Arminius. The Landgrave has

a wild country, he said, but he keeps fine order in it, and
his subjects can go about their business in peace.   He
listens to advice, and when he has made up his mind he
acts promptly, and has taught his enemies to fear him.
If he would give up the Gospel he might ask the Emperor
for what he pleased, and have it.   At Augsburg he said
to the bishops, 'We desire peace.   If you will not have
peace and I must fall, be it so; I shall not fall alone.
The Bishop of Salzburg asked Archbishop Albert why
he was so afraid of the Landgrave, who was but a poor
prince.   'My dear friend,' the Archbishop replied, 'if
you lived as near him as I do, you would feel as I do.'

Singular things were spoken at Augsburg.   A member
of the Diet—his name is not preserved—said, 'If I was
the Emperor I would gather together the best of the
Popish and Lutheran divines, shut them up in a house,
and keep them there till they had agreed.   I would then
ask them if they believed what they had concluded upon
and would die for it; if they said Yes, I would set the
house on fire and burn them there and then to prove their
sincerity.   Then I should be satisfied that they were
right.'

Luther always spoke well of Charles, in spite of the
Edict of Worms.

Strange (he said) to see two brothers like him and Ferdinand so unlike in their fortunes.   Ferdinand always fails.
Charles generally succeeds.   Ferdinand calculates every
detail, and will manage everything his own way.   The
Emperor does plainly and simply the best that he can, and
knows that in many things he must look through his fingers.
The Pope sent him into Germany to root us out and make
an end of us.   He came, and by the grace of God he has left
us where we are.   He is not bloody.   He has true imperial

gentleness and goodness—and fortune comes to him in his sleep. He must have some good angel.

When the Emperor was once in France in time of peace, he was entertained by the king at a certain castle. One night after supper a young lady of noble birth was, by the king's order, introduced into his room. The Emperor asked her who she was and how she came there. She burst into tears and told him. He sent her to her parents uninjured, with an escort and handsome presents. In the war which followed he levelled that castle to the ground.

The Antwerp manufacturers presented him with a tapestry once, on which was wrought for a design the battle of Pavia and the capture of the French king. Charles would not take it. He had no pleasure, he said, in the miseries of others.

Had Luther been a prophet he could have added another story still more to Charles's honour. Years after, when Luther was in his grave, and Charles, after the battle of Muhlberg, entered Wittenberg as a conqueror, some bishop pressed him to tear the body out of the ground and consign it to the flames. He replied, 'I war not with the dead.'

Much as Luther admired Charles, however, his own sovereigns had his especial honour.

The Elector Frederick (he said) was a wise, good man, who hated all display and lies and falsity. He was never married. His life was pure and modest, and his motto, ' Tantum quantum possim,' was a sign of his sense. Such a prince is a blessing from God. He was a fine manager and economist. He collected his own taxes, and kept his accounts strictly. If he visited one of his castles, he was lodged as an ordinary guest and paid his own bills, that his stewards might not be able to add charges for his entertainment. He gathered in with shovels and gave out with spoons. He listened patiently in his council, shut his eyes, and took notes of each opinion. Then he formed his own conclusion ; this

and that advice will not answer, for this and that will come
of it.

Elector John consulted me how far he should agree to
the Peasants' Articles at the time of the rebellion. He said :
'God has made me a prince and given me many horses. If
there is to be a change I can be happy with eight horses or
with four. I can be another man.' He had six young pages
to wait on him. They read the Bible to him for six hours
every day. He often went to sleep, but when he woke he
had always some good text in his mouth. At sermon he took
notes in a pocket-book. Church government and worldly
government were well administered. The Emperor had
only good to say of him. If his brother and he could
have been cast into a single man, they would have made a
wonder between them. The Elector John had a strong frame
and a hard death. He roared like a lion.

John Frederick (reigning elector in the latter part of
Luther's life), though he hates untruth and loose living, is too
indulgent. He fears God and has his five wits about him.
God long preserve him. You never hear an unchaste or dis-
honourable word come out of his lips. One fault he has :
he eats and drinks too much. Perhaps so big a body re-
quires more than a small one. Otherwise he works like a
donkey ; and, drink what he will, he always reads the Bible
before he sleeps.

Luther hated lies as heartily as the Elector. 'Lies,'
he said, 'are always crooked, like a snake, which is never
straight, whether still or moving—never till it is dead—
then it hangs out straight enough.' But he was against
violence, even to destroy falsehood. 'Popery,' he said,
'can neither be destroyed by the sword nor sustained by
the sword ; it is built on lies, it stands on lies, and can
only be overthrown by truth. I like not those who go
hotly to work. It is written, Preach and I will give
thee power. We forget the preaching, and would fly to
force alone.'

He much admired soldiers, especially if besides winning battles they knew how to rule afterwards, like Augustus and Julius Cæsar.

When a country has a good prince over it, all goes well. Without a good prince things go backwards like a crab, and councillors, however many, will not mend them. A great soldier is the man ; he has not many words ; he knows what men are, and holds his tongue ; but when he does speak, he acts also. A real hero does not go about his work with vain imaginations. He is moved by God Almighty, and does what he undertakes to do. So Alexander conquered Persia, and Julius Cæsar established the Roman Empire. The Book of Judges shows what God can do by a single man, and what happens when God does not provide a man. Certain ages seem more fruitful in great men than others. When I was a boy there were many. The Emperor Maximilian in Germany, Sigismund in Poland, Ladislaus in Hungary, Ferdinand, Emperor Charles's grandfather, in Spain—pious, wise, noble princes. There were good bishops too, who would have been with us had they been alive now. There was a Bishop of Wurzburg who used to say, when he saw a rogue, ' To the cloister with you. Thou art useless to God or man.' He meant that in the cloister were only hogs and gluttons, who did nothing but eat, and drink, and sleep, and were of no more profit than as many rats.

Luther knew that his life would be a short one. In his later days he compared himself to a knife from which the steel has been ground away, and only the soft iron left. The Princess Elector said one evening to him : ' I trust you have many days before you. You may live forty years yet, if God wills.' ' God forbid,' Luther answered. ' If God offered me Paradise in this world for forty years I would not have it. I would rather my head was struck off. I never send for doctors. I will not have my life made miserable, that doctors may lengthen it by a twelvemonth.'

The world itself, too, he conceived to be near its end. The last day he thought would be in some approaching Lent, on a ruddy morning when day and night were equal.

The thread is ravelled out, and we are now visibly at the fringe. The present age is like the last withered apple hanging on the tree. Daniel's four Empires—Babylon, Persia, Greece, and Rome—are gone. The Roman Reich lingers; but it is the 'St. John's drink' (the stirrup cup) and is fast departing. Signs in Heaven foretell the end. On earth there is building and planting and gathering of money. The arts are growing as if there was to be a new start, and the world was to become young again. I hope God will finish with it. We have come already to the White Horse. Another hundred years and all will be over. The Gospel is despised. God's word will disappear for want of any to preach it. Mankind will turn into Epicureans and care for nothing. They will not believe that God exists. Then the voice will be heard 'Behold the Bridegroom cometh.'

Some one observed that when Christ came there would be no faith at all on the earth, and the Gospel was still believed in that part of Germany.

'Tush,' he said, ' it is but a corner. Asia and Africa have no Gospel. In Europe, Greeks, Italians, Spaniards, Hungarians, French, English, Poles, have no Gospel. The small Electorate of Saxony will not hinder the end.'

I can but gather specimens here and there out of the four closely-printed volumes of these conversations. There is no such table-talk in literature, and it ought to be completely translated. I must take room for a few more illustrations. Luther was passionately fond of music. He said of it :—

Music is one of the fairest of God's gifts to man ; Satan hates music, because it drives away temptation and evil thoughts. The notes make the words alive. It is the best refreshment to a troubled soul ; the heart as you listen recovers its peace. It is a discipline too ; for it softens us and makes us temperate and reasonable. I would allow no man to be a schoolmaster who cannot sing, nor would I let him preach either.

And again :—

I have no pleasure in any man who, like the fanatics, despises music. It is no invention of ours. It is a gift from God to drive away the devil and make us forget our anger and impurity and pride and evil tempers. I place music next to theology. I can see why David and all the saints put their divinest thoughts into song.

Luther's own hymns are not many; but the few which he composed are jewels of purest water. One of them, the well-known—

Ein' feste Burg ist unser Gott

remains even in these days of Rationalism the National Psalm of Germany. In the last great war the Prussian regiments went into battle chanting it.

Though no one ever believed more intensely in the inspiration of the Bible, he was no worshipper of the mere letter—for he knew that over a large part of Scripture the original text was uncertain. In translating he trusted more to instinctive perception than to minute scholarship. He said :—

I am no Hebraist according to grammar and rules. I do not let myself be tied, but go freely through. Translation is a special gift and grace. A man may know many languages, yet be unable to render one into another. The authors of the Septuagint were not good Hebrew scholars ; St. Jerome was better ; but, indeed, after the Babylonish captivity the language itself was corrupted. If Moses and the prophets rose again they would not understand the words which are given as theirs. When we were translating I gave my assistants these rules :—

Attend to the grammar, but remember

1. Holy Scripture speaks of the words and acts of God.

2. Prefer always in translating the Old Testament a meaning consistent with the New.

He could be critical, too, in his way. His objections to the Epistle of St. James are well known. He says of another book :—'The story of Jonah is more incredible than any poet's fable. If it were not in the Bible I should laugh at it. He was three days in the belly of a great fish ! why, the fish would have digested him in three hours, and converted him into its own flesh and blood. The miracle of the Red Sea was nothing to this. The sequel, too, is so foolish—when he is released he begins to rave and expostulate and make himself miserable about a gourd. It is a great mystery.'

He shared in many of the popular superstitions. He believed in the reality of witchcraft, for instance. The devil he was convinced was personally present—perhaps omnipresent, doing every kind of mischief, and had many times assaulted himself. Many things might thus happen of a strange kind through the devil's agency. Nor was he quick to recognise new scientific discoveries.

'Modern astronomers,' he said, 'pretend that the earth moves, and not the sun and the firmament—as in a carriage or a boat we seem to be motionless ourselves, while the trees and banks sweep past us. These clever fellows will believe nothing old, and must have their own ideas. The Holy Scripture says, Joshua bade the sun stand still, not the earth.'

But his powerful sense and detestation of falsehood gave him an instinctive insight into the tricks of charlatans. He regarded magic as unmixed imposture. He told a story of a Duke Albert of Saxony, to whom a Jew once offered a wonderful gem engraved with strange characters, alleging that it would make the wearer proof against cold steel and gunshot. 'I will try it first on thee,' the Duke said. He took the Jew out of doors with the gem on his neck, and ran his sword through him. 'So it would have been with me,' he said, 'if I had trusted thee."

Astrology, the calculation of a man's fortunes from the place of the planets among the stars, at the time of his birth was an accepted science. Erasmus might doubt, but Erasmus was almost alone in a world of believers. One other doubter was Luther, much to the scandal of his friend Melanchthon, with whom it was an article of faith. Melanchthon showed him the nativity of Cicero.

I have no patience with such stuff (Luther said). Let any man answer this argument. Esau and Jacob were born of the same father and mother, at the same time, and under the same planets, but their nature was wholly different. You would persuade me that astrology is a true science. I shall not change my opinion. I am bachelor, master, and have been a monk. But the stars did not make me either one or the other. It was my own shame that I was a monk, and grieved and angered my father. I caught the Pope by his hair, and he caught me by mine. I married a runaway nun, and begat children with her. Who saw that in the stars? Who foretold that? It is like dice-throwing. You say you have a pair of dice that always throw twice six—

you throw two, three, four, five, six, and you take no notice.
When twice six turns up, you think it proves your case.
The astrologer is right once or twice, and boasts of his art.
He overlooks his mistakes. Astronomy is very well—
astrology is naught. The example of Esau and Jacob
proves it.

They prophesied a flood—another deluge in 1524. No
deluge came, though Burgomaster Hohndorf brought a
quarter-cask of beer into his house to prepare for it. In
1525 was the peasants' insurrection ; but no astrologer prophesied this. In the time of God's anger there was a con-
junction of sin and wrath, which had more in it than
conjunctions of the planets.

I must leave these recorded sayings, pregnant as they
are, and full of character as they are.

I will add but one more. Luther said : 'If I die in
my bed, it will be a grievous shame to the Pope. Popes,
devils, kings, and princes have done their worst to hurt
me ; yet here I am. The world for these two hundred
years has hated no one as it hates me. I in turn have
no love for the world. I know not that in all my life I
have ever felt real enjoyment. I am well tired of it.
God come soon and take me away.'

I return to what remains to be told of Luther's
early life. The storm which threatened Germany hung
off till he was gone. The House of Saxony was divided
into the Ducal or Albertine line and the Electoral or
Ernestine line. Duke Henry dying was succeeded by
the young Maurice, so famous afterwards. Maurice was
a Protestant like the Elector ; but he was intriguing,
ambitious, and unscrupulous. Quarrels broke out between them, which a few years later brought the Elector
to ruin. But Luther, as long as he lived, was able to
keep the peace.

The Council of Trent drew near. After the peace with France, in 1544, the Pope began again to urge the Emperor to make an end of toleration. The free Council once promised, at which the Evangelical Doctors were to be represented, had been changed into a Council of Bishops, to be called and controlled by the Pope, before which the Evangelicals could be admitted only to plead as criminals. How such a Council would decide was not doubtful. The Protestant princes and theologians declined the position which was to be assigned to them, and refused to appear. It was but too likely that, if the peace continued, the combined force of the Empire and of France would be directed against the League of Schmalkald, and that the League would be crushed after all in the unequal struggle.

Luther saw what was coming, and poured out his indignation in the fiercest of his pamphlets. The 'aller heiligst,' 'most holy' Pope, became 'aller höllisch,' 'most hellish.' The pretended 'free Council' meant death and hell, and Germany was to be bathed in blood. 'That devilish Popery,' he said, 'is the last worse curse of the earth, the very worst that all the devils, with all their might, can generate. God help us all. Amen.' Very dreadful and unbecoming language, the modern reader thinks, who has only known the wolf disguised in an innocent sheepskin. The wolf is the same that he was; and if ever he recovers his power, he will show himself unchanged in his old nature. In Luther's time there was no sheepskin; there was not the smallest affectation of sheepskin. The one passionate desire of the See of Rome, and the army of faithful prelates and priests, was to carry fire and sword through every country which had dared to be spiritually free.

E

In the midst of these prospects Luther reached his last birthday. He was tired, and sick at heart, and sick in body. In the summer of 1545 he had wished to retire to his farm, but Wittenberg could not spare him, and he continued regularly to preach. His sight began to fail. In January 1546 he began a letter to a friend, calling himself 'old, spent, worn, weary, cold, and with but one eye to see with.' On the 28th of that month he undertook a journey to Eisleben, where he had been born, to compose a difference between the Counts Mansfelt. He caught a chill on the road, but he seemed to shake it off, and was able to attend to business. He had fallen into the hands of lawyers, and the affair went on but slowly. On the 14th of February he preached, and, as it turned out, for the last time, in Eisleben Church. An issue in the leg, artificially kept open to relieve his system, had been allowed to heal for want of proper attendance. He was weak and exhausted after the sermon. He felt the end near, and wished to be with his family again. 'I will get home,' he said, 'and get into my coffin, and give the worms a fat doctor.'

But wife and home he was never to see again, and he was to pass from off the earth at the same spot where his eyes were first opened to the light. On the 17th he had a sharp pain in his chest. It went off, however; he was at supper in the public room, and talked with his usual energy. He retired, went to bed, slept, woke, prayed, slept again; then at midnight called his servant. 'I feel strangely,' he said; 'I shall stay here; I shall never leave Eisleben.' He grew restless, rose, moved into an adjoining room, and lay upon a sofa. His two sons were with him, with his friend Jonas. 'It is death,' he said; 'I am going: "Father, into Thy hands I commend my spirit."'

Jonas asked him if he would still stand by Christ and the doctrine which he had preached. He said 'Yes.' He slept once more, breathing quietly, but his feet grew cold. Between two and three in the morning he died.

The body lay in state for a day; a likeness was taken of him before the features changed. A cast from the face was taken afterwards; the athlete expression gone, the essential nature of him—grave, tender, majestic—taking the place of it, as his own disturbed life appears now when it is calmed down into a memory. The Elector, John Frederick, hurried to see him; the Counts Mansfelt ended beside his body the controversies which he had come to compose. On the 20th he was set on a car to be carried back to Wittenberg, with an armed escort of cavalry. The people of Eisleben attended him to the gates. The church bells tolled in the villages along the road. Two days later he reached his last resting-place at Wittenberg. Melanchthon cried after him as they laid him in the grave: 'My Father, my Father. The chariot of Israel and the horseman thereof.'

His will, which is extremely characteristic, had been drawn by himself four years before. He left his wife well provided for, and because legal proceedings might be raised upon his marriage, he committed her to the special protection of the Elector. Children, friends, servants, were all remembered.

Finally (he said), seeing I do not use legal forms, I desire all men to take these words as mine. I am known openly in Heaven, on Earth, and in Hell also; and I may be believed and trusted better than any notary. To me a poor, unworthy, miserable sinner, God, the Father of mercy, has entrusted the Gospel of His dear Son, and has made me therein true and faithful. Through my means many in this world have received the Gospel, and hold me as a true teacher, despite of popes, emperors, kings, princes, priests, and all the devil's wrath. Let them believe me also in the small matter of my last will and testament, this being written in my own hand, which otherwise is not unknown. Let it be understood that here is the earnest, deliberate meaning of Doctor Martin Luther, God's notary and witness in his Gospel, confirmed by his own hand and seal.— January 6, 1542.

Nothing remains to be said. Philosophic historians tell us that Luther succeeded because he came in the fulness of time, because the age was ripe for him, because forces were at work which would have brought about the same changes if he had never been born. Some changes there might have been, but not the same. The forces computable by philosophy can destroy, but they cannot create. The false spiritual despotism which dominated Europe would have fallen from its own hollowness. But a lie may perish, and no living belief may rise again out of the ruins. A living belief can rise only out of a believing human soul, and that any faith, any piety, is alive now in Europe, even in the Roman Church itself, whose insolent hypocrisy he humbled into shame, is due in large measure to the poor miner's son who was born in a Saxon village four hundred years ago.

LONDON : PRINTED BY
SPOTTISWOODE AND CO., NEW-STREET SQUARE
AND PARLIAMENT STREET